Craftily EVER AFTER

#8

-- One Big Crafty Family --

By Martha Maker   Illustrated by Xindi Yan

LITTLE SIMON

New York   London   Toronto   Sydney   New Delhi

LITTLE SIMON

An imprint of Simon & Schuster Children's Publishing Division

1230 Avenue of the Americas, New York, New York 10020

First Little Simon hardcover edition May 2021

Copyright © 2021 by Simon & Schuster, Inc.

Also available in a Little Simon paperback edition.

For information about special discounts for bulk purchases, please contact Simon & Schuster Special Sales at 1-866-506-1949 or business@simonandschuster.com.

The Simon & Schuster Speakers Bureau can bring authors to your live event. For more information or to book an event contact the Simon & Schuster Speakers Bureau at 1-866-248-3049 or visit our website at www.simonspeakers.com.

Designed by Leslie Mechanic

The text of this book was set in Caecilia.

Manufactured in the United States of America 0421 FFG

2 4 6 8 10 9 7 5 3 1

This book has been cataloged with the Library of Congress.

ISBN 978-1-5344-6606-7 (hc)

ISBN 978-1-5344-6605-0 (pbk)

ISBN 978-1-5344-6607-4 (eBook)

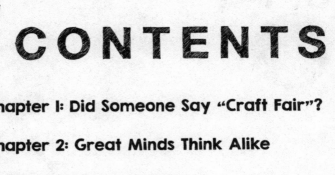

CONTENTS

CHAPTER
1

Did Someone Say "Craft Fair"?

"Bye, Dad!"

Maddie Wilson bounced out of the car in front of Mason Creek Elementary School. Before she had gone two steps, she spotted her three best friends—Bella Diaz, Sam Sharma, and Emily Adams— standing together out front.

At the sight of them, Maddie

practically started cheering. Most weekends, they all got together to work on projects at their craft clubhouse, which they'd created in the shed behind Bella's house. But this weekend, family plans and

homework had kept them apart for
two whole days!

"Hi, guys!" called Maddie,
sprinting over to join her friends.
As she approached, she noticed
that Sam was wearing his
favorite paint-spattered pants,
Emily had on her faded overalls,
which had
holes in the
knees, and
Bella sported
a robotics
team
T-shirt.

Maddie glanced
down at her own
outfit—a top
she'd tie-dyed
and a skirt
she'd made
out of some
fabulous tulle
her mom had
left over from a
job. Maddie's mom
was a seamstress,
which was where Maddie got her
interest in fashion and sewing
from. Maddie looked back up at

her friends and smiled. Who would have guessed that four kids who dressed so differently could become such close friends?

"Hi, guys!" called Maddie, joining the group. "How was everyone's weekend?"

"Great!" Sam told her. "My parents finally let me paint my room."

"Wow," said Emily. "Which color did you choose?"

"All of them!" Sam smiled. "I couldn't decide, so I did a mural of a rainbow."

Just then the school bell rang. The kids walked inside together.

"I can't believe the school year is winding down already," Bella said wistfully.

"I know," agreed Maddie. "Like they say, time flies when you're having fun."

Bella smiled. "Totally! I'm so glad I moved here and met you guys."

"Me too," said Sam. "I mean, I'm glad you moved here, Bella. And I'm also glad I got to know all three of you."

Emily nodded, remembering. "That's right! When school started, Maddie and I didn't know you very well. We just thought of you as that kid who loved to draw."

"I still do," said Sam, pulling out his sketchbook. The friends gathered around to see Sam's latest drawings.

Before long, Ms. Gibbons called the class to order. Maddie tried to focus, but her thoughts kept drifting back to those early days. She remembered when Bella first stood before the class, looking shy but smart and determined. She remembered when Emily first got a peek at the amazing creations inside Sam's sketchbook. And she thought about the day they all went over to Bella's house and explored the shed that would become their beloved craft clubhouse.

Just then Maddie's ears perked up at the sound of two words.

Craft fair?

She looked around. Had she imagined that because she was thinking about the clubhouse?

Or had Ms. Gibbons actually said something about a craft fair?

CHAPTER 2

Great Minds
Think Alike

Standing in the lunch line, Emily looked at Maddie excitedly.

"Can you believe it? In a couple of weeks we're going to have a craft fair at school!"

"And bake sale," added Bella, selecting a carton of milk. "I wonder if my dad has any new recipes we can try." Bella's dad was a chef, so he often shared cooking ideas with Bella and her friends. "He made banana walnut muffins for breakfast and they were banan-tastic!"

"When Ms. Gibbons told us this morning, I thought I dreamed it," admitted Maddie as they carried their trays over to where Sam was sitting.

"Are you guys talking about the craft fair?" asked Sam.

"Yup. It's going to be awesome," said Emily.

"Great minds think alike!" said Sam happily. "I'm so excited. Everyone is going to come and see our work."

"And according to Ms. Gibbons, the money we earn selling our creations will help out the Mason Creek Senior Center," Bella pointed out.

"We've got to come up with something really awesome to make for the fair," said Maddie.

"Oh, we will," Sam assured her. Sam was proud that the four friends had dreamed up so many cool and crafty creations already. They'd made tie-dyed T-shirts, musical instruments, bird feeders, bracelets, piggy banks, garden markers . . .

and so much more. If they could dream it, they could make it!

"Are you thinking what I'm thinking?" Bella asked her friends.

"Meet at the craft clubhouse after school?" asked Sam. All the friends nodded. "See? Great minds!" said Sam triumphantly.

That afternoon, they were going to figure out the *perfect* craft fair project.

Too Many Ideas

The clock in the classroom had to be broken. There was no other explanation for why the day was going by sooooo slooooowly.

Emily couldn't wait to get to the craft clubhouse. It was funny, Emily thought, how much things had changed. When Bella first arrived in their classroom, Emily was convinced she was there to steal her best friend, Maddie. Instead, all three of them had become friends. And they had gotten to know Sam and become friends with him, too!

The other funny thing was how much she and Bella had in common. Sure, Bella liked clicking and clacking on her computer keyboard

and Emily preferred banging and clanging with a hammer and nails, but what they both loved was designing and building. They just used different tools for it!

At long last, the final bell rang and school let out. A little while later, the four friends met up at

Bella's house and sat around the big worktable at the craft clubhouse.

"Okay," said Sam, pulling out his sketchbook. "Whatever we decide to make has to be really special."

"Right!" agreed Bella. "It needs to be something people will really want

to buy, so we can raise as much as possible for the senior center."

"I have the perfect idea!" Maddie stood up and struck a pose. "Bedazzled tops, like the one I'm wearing today. All in favor?"

The others looked at each other.

"Maddie, don't take this the wrong way, but not everyone is as fashion-forward as you are," said Bella. "Though I like the idea of doing something eye-catching. What if we made lava lamps?"

Bella pulled up a website with images and instructions. The others scrutinized the screen.

"Those *are* cool," agreed Sam. "But we'd have to get a lot of glass jars to make them. And they might be hard to transport."

"How about wind chimes?" suggested Emily. "We could use found materials like metal, wood, and various fasteners. Each one could be unique."

"I love the sound of wind chimes," said Maddie. "But . . . not everyone has a yard or somewhere outside to hang them."

"You guys, I've got it," said Sam. The others turned to see that Sam was holding up a sketch of the four friends, grinning. "We can do custom portraits of our customers!"

"Sam, you're the only one who can draw fast enough to do that," Bella pointed out.

Emily looked at Sam's drawing, then at her friends, none of whom were smiling.

Was agreeing on a project going to be harder than they thought?

CHAPTER 4

Going Solo

At lunch the next day, Bella rushed over to join her friends at their usual table.

"After you guys went home last night, I came up with the perfect idea," she announced.

"So did I," said Emily, pulling out a hand-carved wooden whistle and placing it next to her lunch tray.

"Me too," added Maddie. She dug a beaded pot holder out of her backpack.

Sam flipped open his sketchbook to a page that read *Craft Fair Ideas*. The page was covered with notes and doodles. "Me three," he joked. "What's *your* idea, Bella?"

Bella looked around the lunch table. It was great that all four of them were so crafty. Maybe too crafty! Now that she saw her friends' projects, Bella was not so sure that the others would agree on her idea.

"Actually, we have lots of good ideas already," said Bella. "What we really need to do is decide."

"I totally think carved whistles would be a big hit," said Emily. "They're unusual, which makes them special."

"That's true," said Maddie, admiring Emily's woodworking skills. "But I feel like people will only buy one. With pot holders, it's better to have two, one for each hand. Or maybe even three, so you can put one on the table for a hot dish. We'd probably sell a lot."

"Maybe we should take a look at my list," said Sam. "I have lots of ideas here."

There was an awkward silence.

Bella took a deep breath, then spoke again. "I can't believe I'm suggesting this," she said. "But maybe we should each set up our own craft table at the fair?"

Her friends considered this.

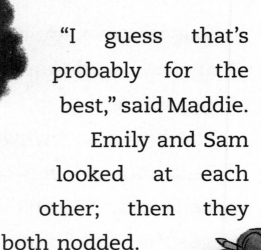

"I guess that's probably for the best," said Maddie. Emily and Sam looked at each other; then they both nodded.

Quietly, Emily put her whistle away. Maddie stowed her pot holder, and Sam packed up his sketchbook. For the first time ever, the friends spent the rest of lunchtime sitting in silence, eating their lunches.

Except for Bella, who suddenly realized she wasn't hungry anymore. It just didn't feel right that after working on so many creative projects together,

they were this *stuck*.

Would they ever find a way to work together again?

CHAPTER
5

Field trip this
Thursday!

Bus Buddies, Not Best Buddies

The next day, when Bella, Sam, Maddie, and Emily entered the classroom, they noticed something new on the board.

Field trip this Thursday!

"Field trip?" Emily asked their teacher.

Ms. Gibbons nodded. "Remember

how I told you that our upcoming craft fair will benefit the senior center? Well, the senior center invited us to visit so we can see the facilities and meet some of the residents."

"Cool!" said Emily. She loved field trips of all kinds.

Her friends nodded in agreement. But something felt . . . off.

At lunch they sat together as usual. But instead of conversation and laughter, there was a lot of awkward silence. Eventually, Maddie pulled out a fashion magazine, Bella got to work on a sudoku puzzle, and Sam began sketching.

Emily sighed. She thought about something she heard Rabbi Stein

say at temple once. "This too shall pass." The rabbi explained that this meant you should stay positive and have faith that things would improve, even in difficult times. *Maybe*, Emily reasoned, *in a day or two, my friends and I will be back in sync again.*

She sure hoped so!

On Thursday afternoon, Ms. Gibbons walked the class outside to get on the bus for the field trip.

"I've paired you up with seating buddies alphabetically," she told her students.

Emily found her buddy and together they boarded the bus and found seats. Because they were among the first pairs, she watched her friends get on the bus with their buddies. They all seemed perfectly

fine. Maddie was chatting happily with her buddy, Sam was showing off his sketchbook, and Bella was examining her seatmate's watch. *Probably programming new functions on it*, thought Emily. She knew Bella couldn't resist new gadgets.

Emily felt a pang of jealousy. It made her think of the day Bella first arrived in their classroom. *This too shall pass*, she reminded herself. Bella, Maddie, and Sam were her best friends and nothing would change that.

Right?

CHAPTER

6

Meet Bruce

"I need your attention, everybody!"

Ms. Gibbons stood at the front of the bus with her clipboard. "Our class is going to split up into groups to tour the center. Each group will be met by a senior resident who will show us around. Listen closely for your name! The first group will get a tour from Bruce. . . ."

Maddie got off the bus when her name was called, then joined the group standing with an older gentleman in a wheelchair. He was wearing a name tag that said BRUCE.

Normally, Maddie would have been so excited to see that her group included Sam, Emily, and Bella. But normally, the four of them would be working *together* on a craft project, not *separately*.

"Hi, kids," said Bruce to the students. "Thanks so much for coming for a visit. My friends and I really appreciate everything you all are doing to help us out. As you'll see, the senior center is more than a home for us. It's a place where we can be together, express ourselves creatively, and feel supported and cared for."

Like the craft clubhouse, thought Maddie. Well, like it used to be.

Bruce rolled along,
leading the way
through the building
and talking as he went.
He showed them the
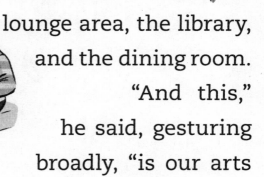
lounge area, the library,
and the dining room.
"And this,"
he said, gesturing
broadly, "is our arts

and crafts room. As
you can see, we
have lots of
space to work.
And many of

us have the background to teach each other about various types of art. For example, I worked as a photographer back in the day. And see my friend Barbara over there? She ran a knitting store and taught weaving."

A woman wearing blue boots and a multicolored shawl waved to the students. Maddie waved back, admiring the older woman's fashion sense.

"This is my favorite place," added Bruce. "Not just in the senior center. But anywhere."

"I know what you mean," said Maddie. "The four of us have a craft clubhouse, where we get together to create cool projects."

"It used to be an old shed," explained Sam. "But we fixed it up ourselves!"

Bruce smiled. "That's wonderful," he said. "There's just one problem with our craft center. With so many folks interested, we keep running out of art supplies."

"Us, too!" said Emily. "But one time we had an agua fresca stand and we raised enough money to buy lots of supplies *and* give some money to charity."

"Agua fresca is like lemonade," explained Bella. "We used my dad's recipe. He's a chef. And the craft clubhouse is in my backyard, so sometimes he brings us homemade treats."

"That sounds delicious," said Bruce. "Our chef here is pretty talented too. Why don't we go check out the café next? If we're lucky, there might be a snack waiting for us."

Maddie, Bella, Sam, and Emily

smiled at each other, then followed Bruce and their group down the hall.

Maybe I'm not the only one who misses being a team, thought Maddie hopefully.

CHAPTER 7

The Spark of an Idea

Bruce was right—it was snack time at the café, and there were all sorts of tasty-looking options. Sam, Maddie, Bella, and Emily made their selections. Then they joined Bruce at a table and told him more about the craft clubhouse.

"One time, we made musical

instruments out of
recycled materials,"
said Sam.

"We've made lots of things,"
added Bella. "Dog
beds, race cars . . .
even robots."

"That's amazing,"
said Bruce. "You kids are clearly
a team of talented and
successful artists."

"We're not always
successful," admitted
Sam. He told the
story of how the four friends

accidentally tie-dyed
Mayor Barnstable's
favorite shirt.
"And it was
right before an
important event,
too!" he added.

"Although the mayor did end up
loving it," Maddie chimed in.

"That wasn't our only mistake,"
said Emily. "Remember the agua
fresca?"

"How could I forget?" said Bella,
groaning. "That first batch was
undrinkable!"

"And Emily's parents were too nice to tell us," said Maddie. Everyone laughed.

"Trial and error is part of every artist's process," said Bruce kindly. "I can't tell you how many blurry photographs I've taken over the years."

"Can we see some of your pictures?" asked Sam.

"Absolutely," said Bruce. "In fact, did you see that big photo in the front lobby?"

"The sunrise?" asked Sam in surprise. "I thought that was a painting, not a photo."

Bruce smiled. "Thanks," he said. "I love taking nature photos. But there's something I like photographing even more."

Bruce pulled out his phone and held the screen up for the group to see.

"This is Audrey, and Charlotte, and Rory," he said. "They're my grandkids."

Sam, Maddie, Emily, and Bella watched as Bruce scrolled through picture after picture.

"Aw," said Maddie. "They must love spending time with you."

Bruce sighed. "Unfortunately, I don't get to see them as often as I'd like. They live very far away."

Suddenly, the look on Bruce's face gave Sam a fantastic idea.

He looked from the phone screen to his friends' faces.

Great minds? he wondered. Could his friends be thinking the exact same thing?

Picture This!

"Ta-da!"

Bella trooped through the craft clubhouse door balancing a tray loaded with fruit, mint agua fresca, and her dad's legendary spicy popcorn. "I hereby call this emergency craft fair meeting to order!" she announced.

Her friends, gathered around the worktable, burst into applause.

"Thanks, Bella!" said Maddie. "I was so happy when you invited us here today. I've missed this so much!"

"Me too," said Emily.

Sam shrugged. "I was doing fine on my own."

The others made faces and threw popcorn at him.

"Okay, okay!" Sam ducked, then grinned. "I missed you guys too."

Bella smiled back. After days

of working solo, it was a relief to discover that she wasn't the only one who preferred crafting with friends. "Besides, Sam, you really did come up with the perfect craft fair project."

"I know," agreed Emily. "I've already started making the frames."

"And I'll take care of painting them every color of the rainbow," said Sam.

"And I'm going to decorate them!" said Maddie.

"Translation: she's going to bling them out like nobody's business," joked Bella.

"Maybe *some* of them," admitted Maddie. "But I know that's not everyone's style. I promise I'll do a range of patterns and themes.

There'll be something for everyone."

"Wait, what about you, Bella?" asked Sam, a concerned look on his face.

Bella held up her tablet and smiled. "I'll show you. Say cheese!"

With the tablet, Bella snapped a handful of photos of her friends,

individually and together. Then, using her tablet, she organized them into a digital collage. She also incorporated words in the composition: all of their names, "craft clubhouse" and, of course, "BFFs."

"Wow, that looks amazing, Bella!" said Sam. The others nodded in agreement.

"Thanks!" Bella used the controls to adjust the lighting. "Remember how Bruce had all those pictures of his grandkids on his phone? My mom's the same way with pictures of me and my brother. I figured people might like a way to see several pictures at once."

"So, if customers want, they can email you their photos?" asked Maddie.

Bella nodded. "Exactly. With my tablet and printer and the templates I've designed, I can help our customers make and print digital collages to go in their frames."

"That's awesome," said Emily. "Speaking of frames, we've actually got to make a bunch of them if we want to be ready for the craft fair."

"You're right," said Maddie, grabbing one last handful of popcorn. "Let's get crafting!"

The friends cleared off the table and formed an assembly line. As Emily finished assembling a frame, she handed it to Sam. Maddie gathered crafting supplies and planned out design patterns until Sam's creations were dry. Then she began adding rhinestones, beads, and other festive decorations to the frames.

Bella sat on the other side of the clubhouse because her job involved a lot of focus. On her tablet, she designed several templates. Then, using her own photos, she created examples to show people ways to customize their collages. She was so involved in her work that she was surprised when she suddenly heard her name.

"Hey, Bella! Look!"

Bella looked up and saw her friends, each holding up a colorful decorated frame and making a silly face inside it.

Bella burst out laughing.

She was so happy to be back in the craft clubhouse, surrounded by her friends. She couldn't wait to take their creations to the craft fair that coming weekend.

CHAPTER 9

A Photo Finish

"Emily! Hey, Emily! Over here!"

Emily could hear her friends calling her name. She just couldn't see them because the box of frames she was carrying was so big.

Bella, Maddie, and Sam ran over to help. Maddie grabbed the other side of Emily's box, while

Sam and Bella went outside to find Emily's parents' car and unload more picture frames.

When Bella and Sam returned, they saw that Emily and Maddie had already arranged a wonderful display of the various colors, sizes, and options. Then Sam pulled out a big poster and hung it up so everyone could see what they were offering. And Bella set up her printer and made sure her tablet was connected to the Wi-Fi network so she could accept digital payments and print collages.

Then, when everything was
set, the friends began to wait for
customers.

Emily looked at the tables on either side of them. On their left was a table with mouthwatering baked goods. And on their right was a display of handmade ceramic coffee cups with delicate flower designs.

Emily began to worry. Her mom drank a lot of coffee and collected interesting mugs. And her dad never met a cookie he didn't like.

What if no one wants or needs a picture frame?

"Aren't these darling!"

Emily thought the woman must have been talking about the coffee mugs. But when she looked up, she saw that the customer was holding a frame and admiring it.

"Thanks," said Emily, smiling shyly. "My friends and I made them."

"What a great idea," said the woman. "All my picture frames are so boring. These are so happy and colorful! I'll take two."

Emily was so excited she didn't know what to say.

Luckily, Bella did. "Cash or charge?" she asked, holding up her tablet.

Just then a man came up to their table. He showed the frames to his wife, and she bought one. And another man came over and bought two. The customers lined up for Bella to help them.

Emily replaced the sold picture frames with others from their supply as more customers gathered.

Their picture frames were a hit! Then, above the buzz of conversation, Emily heard a familiar voice.

"Hey there, kids!"

It was Bruce, holding one of their picture frames.

"Hi, Bruce!" said Sam, coming over, along with Maddie. "What a cool surprise."

"It's so good to see you," added Maddie.

"You too!" said Bruce. "When I saw that the senior center was organizing a trip to the craft fair, I signed up right away. I love the chance to check out other artists' work. And I knew whatever you kids were making would be impressive."

"We were actually inspired by you," Emily told him. "You love taking photographs, and you love your grandkids. So we decided to bring the two things together."

"I'm honored," said Bruce. "But I need to tell you something. I'm not here just as an admirer."

"You're not?" asked Sam.

Bruce shook his head, then smiled. "I'm here as a customer. I'll take three!"

One Big Crafty Family

Knock, knock!

"Hey, Bella, you in there? Open up—it's us! We gathered all the materials to make that puppet theater we talked about at school. But they weigh a ton and we're about to drop them!"

"Hold your horses. I'm coming!"

Bella ran over and threw open the door to the craft clubhouse.

"What took you so long?" asked Sam, carrying in an armload of painting supplies.

"I was working on something," said Bella.

"Can we see?" asked Emily, setting down an armload of wood with a clatter.

"In a little while, sure," replied Bella.

"So secretive," joked Maddie, unloading two overflowing bags of fabric scraps. "Is it a surprise?"

"Maybe," said Bella. "Speaking

of surprises, how cool was it to surprise Bruce and his friends at the senior center last week?"

"I know!" Maddie grinned. "Could you believe how different their arts and crafts room looked from the first time we visited?"

"It was like night and day!" agreed Sam. "The first time, there were just one or two people, and almost no materials on the shelves."

"But now it's like a party in there!" said Emily. She smiled at the memory. "I couldn't believe how many activities they had going on at once. A birdhouse-making club, a tai chi class, a batik workshop . . ."

"And the tools," gushed Bella. "That 3D printer they have is amazing!"

"I know. And I can't believe Bruce said we were welcome anytime *and* that we might be able to teach some classes there if we want," added Maddie.

"Maybe when we finish making our puppet theater, we could bring it there and put on a show?" suggested Sam.

"Great minds!" said Bella, smiling back at Sam. "I was thinking the exact same thing."

Just then, the printer started

buzzing. Bella ran over to take a look.

"Hey, guys?" she called over her shoulder. "Close your eyes."

Maddie, Emily, and Sam looked

at each other, but then they did as
Bella asked.

"No peeking!" Bella said.

They heard her rummaging
around as the printer continued
spitting out prints.

Finally, they heard Bella's voice

again. "Okay, now you can open your eyes."

Her friends lowered their hands and saw that in front of each of them was a colorful painted frame. A purple sparkly one for Maddie, a blue geometric design for Emily, and a yellow sunburst pattern for Sam.

"Are these the frames we had left over from the craft fair?" asked Sam.

"Yup, they're the only ones we had left—those three and this one." Bella held up a red-and-black striped frame, which she had selected for herself.

"Wait, these are for us?" Emily

asked. She had just noticed the
image in the frame. It was a
collage of photographs of her and

her friends: Emily, Sam, Bella, and Maddie on the day they finished converting the shed into the craft clubhouse. Sam and Bella chasing their homemade race cars. Emily and Maddie with the mayor at the community garden's grand opening. And one of all of them at the craft fair, gathered around Bruce's wheelchair.

"Wow, these are awesome!" said Sam, admiring the collage.

"Totally," agreed Maddie. "We look like one big family!"

Bella smiled. It was hard to

believe that not so long ago, the craft clubhouse was just an old shed in her backyard. It was exciting to see how things could be transformed with a little imagination and a lot of teamwork. It had been hard, but it was worth it.

And she was especially glad that, because of the craft fair, they had all realized the same thing: that whatever they did, it would be better if they did it together.

Maddie's voice interrupted her thoughts. "Are you guys ready to start hemming curtains for our puppet theater?" she asked.

"Shouldn't we paint the theater first?" asked Sam.

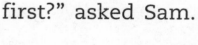

"In order to paint it, we need to finish constructing it," Emily pointed out.

"Don't you mean *start* constructing it?" joked Maddie, pointing at the pile of wood.

"Okay, everyone. Let's get crafting!" said Bella.

The four friends grabbed their tools and materials and got to work. They sawed, sanded, sewed, and painted, excited to see their vision come to life. As they worked, they took turns, helped each other,

cheered each other on, laughed, and joked.

Just like one big family, thought Bella happily.

One big crafty *family.*

How to Make . . .
A Picture Frame

What you need:

A photo!
Cardboard (a cereal box works great)
Acrylic paint
Paintbrush
Craft supplies: sequins or gems, glitter or glitter glue,
buttons, etc.
Scissors or X-Acto knife
Glue

 For the front of your picture frame, you'll want
a piece of cardboard that's slightly larger than
your photo.

Step 2: Trace your photo on the cardboard, then cut out a piece that's a bit bigger than that. If you are going to use an X-Acto knife, have an adult help you.

Step 3:

To make a window in your frame, take that piece of cardboard and draw a rectangle that's slightly *smaller* than your photo. Cut that rectangle out.

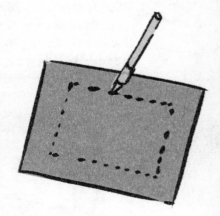

Step 4: Decorate the frame! Paint it, then add any other decorations you want.

Cut one last piece of cardboard that's a tiny bit smaller than the front of the frame. This will be the back of the frame.

Step 5: To glue the front and back of the frame together, put glue on the unpainted side of the front of the frame. Only put glue on three sides—leaving the fourth side as it is. Then stick the front of the frame to the back of the frame

Step 6: When the paint and glue are dry, slide your photo into the unglued side of the frame!

If you like Craftily Ever After, then you'll love . . .

HE.D.i HECKELBECK

the adventures of
SOPHiE MOUSE

the adventures of · 1
SOPHiE MOUSE
A New Friend
by Poppy Green · illustrated by Jennifer A. Bell

the adventures of · 2
SOPHiE MOUSE
The Emerald Berries
by Poppy Green · illustrated by Jennifer A. Bell

the adventures of · 3
SOPHiE MOUSE
Forget-Me-Not Lake
by Poppy Green · illustrated by Jennifer A. Bell

the adventures of · 4
SOPHiE MOUSE
Looking for Winston
by Poppy Green · illustrated by Jennifer A. Bell

the adventures of · 5
SOPHiE MOUSE
The Maple Festival
by Poppy Green · illustrated by Jennifer A. Bell

the adventures of · 6
SOPHiE MOUSE
Winter's No Time to Sleep
by Poppy Green · illustrated by Jennifer A. Bell

the adventures of · 7
SOPHiE MOUSE
The Clover Curse
by Poppy Green · illustrated by Jennifer A. Bell

the adventures of · 8
SOPHiE MOUSE
A Surprise Visitor
by Poppy Green · illustrated by Jennifer A. Bell

the adventures of · 9
SOPHiE MOUSE
The Great Big Paw Print
by Poppy Green · illustrated by Jennifer A. Bell